MW00508440

The Kelly's Family Secrets

Patsy Wallace

Copyright © 2020 Patsy Wallace
All rights reserved
First Edition

NEWMAN SPRINGS PUBLISHING
320 Broad Street
Red Bank, NJ 07701

First originally published by Newman Springs Publishing 2020

ISBN 978-1-64801-791-9 (Paperback)
ISBN 978-1-64801-792-6 (Digital)

Printed in the United States of America

ACKNOWLEDGMENTS

I want to thank God for the gift of being creative in writing poems and stories. My grandson, Ethan, told me not to give up in writing my story. Ben, my grandson, helped me with my computer, and I thank him for that. I thank my friend, Allena, for helping me too. My husband, Jerry, my daughter, Betty, and her husband, Phillip, all have encouraged me as well.

CHAPTER 1

Where's the Leg?

"Bob Kelly, you must keep our family secrets," said his mother, Kitty Ann Kelly. She had a coughing spell. She had a visit this morning from her doctor, Mr. Smith. The news wasn't good; her heart was slowing down. Her time was running out, and she knew it would be over soon. Her son had to know where the leg was buried.

"Bob, are you listening to me?" She tried to reach for her water glass on the table.

"What family secrets are you talking about?" asked Bob. He reached for her glass for her.

"I'm not talking about Irish stories. It's about you, bringing that coffin here to be buried on our family cemetery. He was not a Kelly!"

"Mom, I told you over and over that I never kill him."

His daughter, Kitty Kelly, was walking up the stairs when she heard her father say, "I never kill him."

Kelly couldn't believe what she was hearing. Her father couldn't kill anyone because he was the kindest father anyone could have.

Kitty had to hear more. She didn't want her mother, Ann, to discover her in the hallway, listening. Kitty crawled on her knees to the open bedroom door.

She quickly slipped under her grandmother's bed without anyone seeing her.

"Bob, you must never tell anyone our family secrets." Kitty Ann was exhausted. She could feel her heart beating faster. "Please, Bob, you have to find that leg!"

"So you can give the leg to the museum?" Bob shook his head. He had read her will. He would never give the leg to the people to come and see it. He had hid it good. The truth was he forgot where.

Tears were running down Kitty Ann's checks. "Something bad will happened to the family if you don't get rid of that man buried in my land."

"Mother, I know you've been mad at me for bringing his coffin here, but—" Bob stopped talking. He walked to the door. "It's too late to do anything." He opened the door. "Mom, I have to get up early to milk the cows. I'm tired."

"If I'm still here," said his mother. "Please, Bob, tell me also why you married Ann. She is not a good mother to Kitty."

"I needed a mother for Kitty, and Ann needed a home." He went out the bedroom. Bob slammed the door close. He didn't know what he was going to do with his mother. She was getting harder for them to take care of. He didn't want to bring Ann's husband's coffin with him, but he didn't have any money to get home from Alaska.

Bob sat down in his chair and lit up his favorite pipe. He wondered if he could remember where he had buried the leg. Was it buried here on this farm? Or at the old cabin near the forest? *Oh well*, he thought, *it can stay where it is forever.*

He had many more secrets that he didn't want anyone to know.

Kitty knew she had to quickly find a way to get out of her grandmother's room before her father came upstairs to kiss her goodnight. She was glad Grandma was sleeping. Kitty quickly crawled out from under the bed.

The bedroom door had a squeak in it. Kitty knew that her grandmother would awake up.

How was she going to get out of the room? Kitty walked over to the door. "Lord, I need a miracle." Suddenly, the door was open. Kitty heard her father's footstep coming upstairs.

She hurried to her room and climbed into her bed. She pulled her quilt up to her neck.

Bob knocked on Kitty's bedroom door. "Kitty." He opened the door.

"Yes, Daddy, I am still awake." Kitty yawned.

Bob had promised his wife he would give their child a kiss on her forehead every night. He still cries when he thinks of what happened to her.

"I'm not a little child anymore, Daddy." Kitty smiled. "I'm sixteen. I can get married now." Kitty knew she was in love with Carl Carlson since the first grade. He's the nicest boy in the school.

"You're too young even to think of getting married. I saw you and Carl dancing together at the party." Bob reached out to touch her hand. "Wait for the right man to come along."

Kitty wanted to tell her father that she loved Carl. "Good night, Daddy."

"You will always be my little kitten because I love you." Bob kissed her forehead.

Kitty smiled. "I love you too." Then she watched him walked out of her room. Bob closed her bedroom door. Kitty got out of bed quickly and changed into her nightgown. Then she jumped into her bed.

Kitty heard an Irish voice saying, "Shame on you for listening." Kitty looked around the room.

"I'm down here on the floor," said a man's voice.

Kitty looked down to see an older little man with a white long beard. He had on a green suit with a black tie.

"Who are you!" cried Kitty. She was scared, but he was so little, she could step on him. "Were you listening too?" She sat up in her bed. "Where in the world did you come from?"

"One guess," said the elf as he danced an Irish jug.

"You didn't come from Ireland in one day," said Kitty.

"No, I came with Kitty Ann. You were named after her." He was out of breath. He sat down on the floor to rest. "My brother, John, is a better dancer than me. He's younger than me, but I am the boss. You better tell your father to listen to his mother."

"He's very stubborn person," said Kitty. "Where you in grandmother's bedroom too?"

7

"I was under the bed with you, listening."

"Shame on you for listening too," said Kitty. Kitty closed her eyes; she was thinking that she was dreaming.

Suddenly, Kitty felted a pinch on her arm. She cried out to the elf, but he was gone. Kitty covered herself with her beautiful quilt and was fast to sleep.

It was dark when Grandma was yelling, "Bring me the potty."

Kitty opened her blue eyes, then she heard Grandma cried out, "Kitty, I need that potty now!"

Kitty jumped out of bed and ran to her grandmother's room. She helped Grandma get out of bed. Her father had made a hole in one of the older chairs. It had a metal pail under it.

"Thanks, Kitty," said Grandma as she finished wiping her butt.

She winked her blue Irish eyes and said, "Someone told me that you were under my bed listening when I was talking to your father." Grandma stood up, and Kitty helped her to bed.

"Who were you talking to?" asked Kitty. "It sounded like an Irish old man." She wanted to ask her grandmother about the leg. Was it a human or an animal?

Grandma smiled. "My dear little friends tell me everything." She covered herself with her quilt. "It's too early to talk. Go to bed."

Kitty walked to her bedroom and climbed back to bed.

Tomorrow was the first day of school. She knew that Carl liked her. He smiled at her a lot with his cute dimple. She couldn't wait to see him. Kitty closed her eyes and was dreaming about Carl until her mother was hitting Kitty's arm.

"Get up, lazy bones," said Kitty's mother, Ann. "You must do your chores before you go to school." She walked over to a hook on the wooden wall. She pulled off a white dress that she had made for Kitty. "Put this on." She grabbed Kitty's school dress.

Kitty got out of bed and picked up the dress. She had tears in her eyes. "They will make fun of me at school."

She put on her brown dress that she wears to feed the animals. Kitty heard her mother's voice. She ran down the stars to the kitchen.

"You don't have time to eat," said Ann. "Go feed the animals."

Kitty opened the door to go outside. She walked into the barn, where her father was milking the cows. "Good morning! I feed the chickens and the pigs for you because it was your first day of school." Her father hugged her. Then he told her to stay away from Carl.

"Why?" said Kitty. "He's the nicest boy in the class."

Bob didn't know how to tell Kitty that boys have "things" on their mind. He cleared his throat. "It's best you don't get serious with him."

"But Carl is my friend since we were toddlers."

"People are talking about you two kids."

Kitty couldn't believe what her father was saying. "Why?"

"Kitty, you better get ready for school," said Bob. "We can talk about this later."

She turned around and went out of the barn.

Her favorite cat followed her to a swing in the yard. Kitty sat down to cry. Then she heard her mother yelling at her to get ready for school. Her mother had a temper. Kitty knew she better hurried up the steps to her bedroom. Pulling on the dress that was too big for her, she thought, *I rather go nude to school then wear this ugly thing.*

Kitty washed up and brushed her long reddish hair. Then she went downstairs, hoping to eat something. But one look at her mother, she wasn't going to.

Kitty reached for her lunch pail and hurried out of the house. She walked down the path that led to the wooden fence where her friends, Carl, Sarah, and Billy, would be waiting for her.

Around the bend, she saw Carl first. He was waving at her.

Kitty waved back to him. She wanted to run into his arms and tell him all her problems but not about that little man. That was a secret she must keep.

"Where did you get that dress?" asked Sarah. She walked around Kitty with a grin on her face. "Who made that?"

"My mother," said Kitty as she looked down at the ground.

"It probably was hers when she was sixteen," said Billy.

"I think you look pretty," said Carl with a smile.

"Let's go to school," said Sarah. "Before we are late."

The schoolhouse was outside of the town about a mile away. They heard the school bell. They started to run to the schoolhouse. Kitty tripped on her long dress and fall. Carl was there to help her up. He held her a few seconds, enough to make Kitty's heartbeat faster. Carl asked her if she was okay; she nodded yes.

Their teacher was Miss Howard, and all the students liked her. She made learning interesting.

"So happy to see all my students today," said Miss Howard. "We got a lot to learn today, so let's get started with spelling."

It was Kitty's favorite's subject; she had no trouble with words. Her mind wasn't on what Ms. Howard was saying. It was on the snickering about her dress.

"Is Kitty getting married?" Billy asked his teacher with a grin.

"I don't know, maybe someday," said Miss Howard.

"We know who she's going to marry," said Sarah. She turned and looked at Carl. Everyone looked at Carl, except Kitty. She had her head down.

Miss Howard rang the bell for recess. She told Kitty to wait a minute. When all the students were outside, Miss Howard went to her wooden desk and got some safely pins. "Kitty, let me pin up your dress so you can walk better."

"I hate this dress," said Kitty. She had tears in her blue eyes.

Miss Howard gave her a little hug. "Someday you'll have beautiful dresses."

"Thanks," said Kitty. "I want to be a teacher like you."

The students were waiting for Kitty to come out of the schoolhouse.

"That's not all we know," said Sarah. "My mother told me that she heard that the crazy, old Irish woman talks to little men."

"And everyone laughs at her when she comes to town," said Billy. He grinned and remarked to Kitty, "Do you talk to little men too?"

Carl had enough of their unkindness to the girl he loved.

"Stop it, Billy," said Carl. "Say you're sorry to Kitty."

"Why?" said Billy. "It's not a secret in town. It's the truth."

"You don't have to be mean about it," said Carl. He glanced over to Kitty's who had tears running down her checks.

"You two are lovers," said Billy. "Do you have to get married?"

Carl was taller than Billy and stronger too. He hit Billy in his right eye. Billy screamed so loud that Miss Howard came running out of the schoolhouse.

Billy was on the ground, crying. "Carl did it. I'm going to be blind in this eye. I have to go to my father. He's a doctor. He knows what to do."

Carl said, "I hope, he knows how to spank you too."

Miss Howard announced to the students that she will take Billy to his father. "Carl, you're older. You should know better than to hit." She helped Billy up from the ground. "Everyone can go home." Billy was crying louder. "Carl, hitch up the horses to the wagon."

Carl wanted to walk Kitty home instead. He drove the two horses up to the schoolhouse.

"Carl, we will talk about this later," said Ms. Howard.

CHAPTER 2

A Sad Day

This was the worse day of Kitty's life. She sat on the fence, waiting for Carl. Then she saw Carl running to her.

"I'm sorry," she told him, "now you're in trouble at home."

"My father will say after he hears the story, 'You should have taken both eyes out.' Everyone knows that Billy is a spoiled brat."

"Are you okay?" He pulled Kitty toward him. He looked at her sad face. Then his lips touched hers, so gentle and so soft. Kitty could have melted in his arms. She kissed him back. They didn't know that Sarah was watching them kissing.

"Wow! You two are really lovers," said Sarah. She couldn't wait to tell her mother; she took off running home.

"Now the whole town will be talking about us," said Kitty. "My father said they're talking. But I don't understand why?"

"Let's get married," said Carl. "We'll have a big family."

Kitty pulled away quickly. Getting married was fine, but a big family like his nine siblings? No way.

Carl pulled her back into his strong arms. "I know you love me." He planted another strong kiss on her lips. Kitty felt it down to her toes. She could hardly breath. Kitty could feel Carl pull her down to the ground. His hands were touching her dress.

She pushed Carl's away from her and said, "I want to wait until I'm older to get married."

"I'm sorry, Kitty, I guess I was in a hurry." He helped her up from the ground. He brushed the dirt off her white dress.

"I'd better go home," said Kitty. She took off running down the path.

When Kitty got closer to house, she saw Dr. Smith's wagon by the house. He was coming out of the door, carrying his black bag.

She ran up to him and said, "Did my grandmother die?"

Dr. Smith touched her shoulder. "No, not today. She needs more rest. I'll be back tomorrow to check up on her." He walked over to his horse.

Kitty ran inside the house; her mother was taking out the fresh bread. It smelled so good. She wished her mother would talk more to her. So many questions she needed to know.

Ann handed Kitty a wooden tray with a cup of tea and bread. "Take this tray up to your grandmother."

Kitty heard her father talking loudly to his mother. The door was open.

"Put that tray down and get out of here. Your father and I must have a serious talk," said Grandma. She was holding her hand over her heart. She was in pain, but this talk must be now.

Kitty put the tray down on the table. She quickly went out in the hallway. She heard father say, "You didn't need to be so rude.

"I don't want her to know the Kelly's family secrets until she is older."

"What about your dear friends?" said Bob Kelly. "They know more than I do." He sat down on the bed. "Okay, Mother, let's get this over with so I can get my work done."

"You care more about your work, then you do about me dying."

"Mother, I love you, and I can't take all these secrets," said Bob. He put his hands over his eyes. "I'm having trouble sleeping."

"That's because you're guilty of killing Ann's husband. And—"

"How many times do I have to tell you I didn't kill him." Bob stood up.

"You know who did it?" said his mother. "Is it someone we know?"

"It's a secret you'll never find out or your elves." Bob came nearer to her. "And what, Mother? You're mad because I took a bad woman in your house?"

"I'm mad because you buried her husband in my family cemetery."

"When you die, I'll bury you right next to him. By the way, what happened to my father? What secrets are you keeping? Let's get them out before you die." Bob walked back and forth in the room. "I had to bring Ann's husband's coffin. I didn't have a choice." He stopped talking. "If she knew that there was a baby in coffin too, she would had shot me."

"Did you tell Kitty yet about her mother?" asked his mother.

"Like you said, she's too young to know all our secrets."

"What about the leg? I had promised the state of Washington that I would give it to them."

"How do you know for sure was its Bigfoot's?" said Bob.

"My father told me that the Indians told him about the huge bears in the forests. They all call the huge bears that name."

"And your father gave the leg to me to hide from you. I was only ten years old when he helped me buried it." Bob shook his head. He knew you would give it to the scientists to study.

"Did you find out who the father is of—"

Bob stood up and said to his mother, "That's another secret you'll never know."

"There's some secrets that we have to take to our graves," said his mother. Kitty Ann Kelly had a coughing spell. Bob said, "I'll sent up some hot tea."

"No, I'm exhausted. There's one more secret about your father, but I'm too tired now, perhaps tomorrow if I am still here."

Kitty was in the kitchen when her father came downstairs. She watched him walk outside to smoke his pipe. He looked so tired. She didn't dare listen to them.

"Where are you going with that buttermilk?" said Ann. "You never drink it."

14

"I'm learning to like it now," said Kitty. "I'm going to my bedroom and do my homework." She walked up the stairs to her room. First thing she saw was two little men lying on her bed.

"Great, you got us some buttermilk," said John. He licked his lips.

"Not until you tell me what you heard, listening to my father and my grandmother," said Kitty. She put the glass of buttermilk on the table.

"We didn't learn where the leg was," said Barney.

"They just ask each other questions," said John. "Nothing new."

Kitty heard her father calling for her to come to the kitchen. "Now!"

"It sounds like you're in trouble," said John.

Kitty walked very slow down the stairs to the kitchen. She said hello to Dr. Smith. She wondered if he was here for Grandma or to tell her father about Billy's eye. Dr. Smith went upstairs.

"Dr. Smith told me what happened at school today. Carl got in trouble. He was fighting with Billy. He should know better than to pick on a young boy."

Kitty wanted to tell her father what happened.

"I told you Carl was too young to be married. He's got a bad temper."

"Dad, I must go and feed the animals." Kitty went out the door and walked to the barn. "Here, Princess, here, Princess."

Nowhere to be found. She went to the milk room, no cat there.

Her mother would never let Princess inside the house. Kitty asked her once if she could bring Princess to her room. Ann told her if I did, she would kill the cat.

It was getting dark; Kitty came inside for supper. She asked her father if he saw Princess. He said no. He looked at Ann. "Did you see the cat?"

"I told her if I found the cat in the house. What I would do?"

Kitty's face turned pale. She dropped her fork. "You didn't."

"Did you?" asked Bob. "You know Kitty loves that cat."

"I told her what I would do," said Ann.

Kitty ran upstairs to her bedroom. "Why is my mother so mean?"

"Don't cry, Kitty," said Barney. "He is out chasing his girlfriends."

"He's making kittens," said John. He threw his head back and laughed.

"I thought Princess was a girl," said Kitty. "Now I'll call him Prince."

Ann opened Kitty's bedroom door. "How did this dress get so dirty?" Her brown eyes got darker. "You were rolling in the hay."

"No," said Kitty. "I had fallen down walking to school."

"Don't lie to me," said Ann. She struck Kitty's in the face with her hand.

Then she turned and walk out of Kitty's room.

After school, Carl told Kitty at recess that he couldn't walk her home for a week because Ms. Howard said that he would have to stay after school.

He touched Kitty's arm. "I would rather walk you home." He kissed her on her lips.

Kitty said, "It was my fault." She kissed him back. "I better go home. My mother will be wanting me." She hurried down the path to the wooden fence toward home. She saw her father walking to the barn. She followed him. When he looked at her, he had tears in his eyes.

"What's wrong?" Kitty ran into his arms.

"Grandma is dead," said Bob. He took the saddle off the post. "I'll have to go over to Carlson's. Rose will help me." Bob put the saddle of his horse. Kitty watched him ride away. She knew that her father went to school with Rose.

Walking in the house and slowly went upstairs, Kitty went to her room. She threw herself on her bed. And sobbed.

Barney and John were sitting on the pillow. They were sad.

"Don't cry, Kitty," said Barney. "She's not dead."

"She's not?" said Kitty as she quickly sat up. "Dad said she was."

"We will see her again," said John. "Do you want to see her now?"

Kitty shook her head. Tears were flowing from her eyes. She loved her grandmother. "Dead people don't talk."

Kitty cried until she fell asleep. Awake up, she heard Rose's voice. She looked out her window. Carl was talking to his father. She walked down the steps to the kitchen. Rose greeted her with a hug. Ann and Rose went upstairs to wash Grandma's body and to put on her best dress. Kitty saw Carl on the swing. She wanted to run into his arms. She walked over to him.

"Sorry," said Carl. He got up and took her in his arms.

"We knew Grandma was dying," said Kitty. She saw Ann and Rose coming out of the house. Kitty pulled away from Carl. Ann saw her and gave her a dirty look.

"We have the funeral tomorrow early in the morning," said Bob. "Thanks for coming." Rose gave him a hug.

They watched them drive away before they came into the house. Ann took out the cheese and fresh bread for supper. "Oh, by the way, Kitty, I'm moving Grandma's stuff to the barn. You'll be sleeping in her room."

Kitty opened her mouth to say that she loved her room. It wasn't worth arguing with Ann. Her father always sided in with Ann. Why? Could he speak up?

Kitty ate in silent; she wasn't hungry. She couldn't control her grief. She got up and ran up the stars. Kitty walked slowly past Grandma's room. She opened the bedroom door. Grandma looked pretty in her favorite dress. She looked peaceful.

"I'm peaceful," said a voice behind her. Kitty saw her grandmother.

"Grandma!" Kitty couldn't believe her eyes.

"It's the luck of the Irish," said Grandma. "I'm an Irish ghost." She laughed and disappeared.

Kitty rubbed her eyes. "I can't tell anyone, or they'll lock me up."

CHAPTER 3

Grandma's Funeral

In the morning, Ann had bread and jam to eat for breakfast. Bob was tired. He had stayed up all night making grandmother's wooden coffin. He didn't say a word. Kitty sat down to eat.

Ann looked out the window and said, "The Carlson's are here." Kitty opened the door for them. Bob got up when Carl Senior and his son, Carl, came in the room.

"The coffin is ready. It's in the barn. I have my wagon ready to go."

"Good," said Carl Senior. "Let's go." The men walked to the barn and loaded the coffin onto Bob's wagon. Bob drove the wagon up to the house. Then the men went upstairs to get Kitty Ann Kelly's body. They carried it down the stairs to Bob's wagon.

"Kitty, you will ride up with me," said her father. He helped her up.

"Where are we going?" asked Kitty. Her father wasn't talking.

The little parade went into the deep forest until they came to a small cabin. They pulled the wagons around the backside of the house, where many graves were. Bob helped Kitty down from the wagon. Someone had dug the grave. Kitty walked around the small cemetery. She recognized her great-grandparents names on the crosses. It was 1857 that Robert Kelly died. His wife died the next year.

Kitty stopped in her track when she saw a grave without a name but craved on a wooden cross was written, I WAS MURDERED.

Was this the grave of the man who was murdered. Her grandmother asked her father, "Did you murder him?"

"Kitty, I called you twice," said Carl. "They're ready to say a prayer."

The coffin was in the grave hole. She went to her father's side. Bob started, "Our Father," and they all said it together.

Bob told everyone thanks for coming and helping him. Everyone shook his hand. Bob and Carl's father covered the coffin with dirt.

Kitty was talking to Rose. "Why is this grave without a name?" She pointed to the sign, I WAS MURDERED. Rose said she didn't know. "And where is my grandfather's grave?"

"I think he's in Seattle," said Rose. She was hoping that Kitty wouldn't see Carolina's headstone. They heard Bob saying, "Let's go home."

It was a quiet ride out of the forest. So many questions she wanted to ask her father about. They pasted Carlson's and waved goodbye. Kitty waved at Carl.

"I told you not to get serious with Carl," said her father without looking at her.

"Dad, we love each other," said Kitty. She had tears in her blue eyes. "I don't think my mother loves me."

Bob stopped the wagon at the house to help Kitty down from the wagon.

"Ann had a rough life in Alaska. She doesn't know how to love because—" He stopped talking and drove the wagon to the barn. He liked Carl. He would make a good husband for Kitty.

Bob had to do what Ann told him to do. Or she would tell Kitty that she wasn't her mother. Kitty walked slowly up the stairs to her room. She stopped; it wasn't hers. She didn't want to sleep in grandmother's room. She opened the door. It had a cold feeling. Kitty wanted to run away, but where would she go?

Kitty saw a vase with some wildflowers; she wonders who put them here.

"We put the flowers there," said Barney. "We wanted you to be happy."

"Happy!" said Kitty with tears flowing down her face. "Grandma is dead."

"No, I'm not dead," said Grandma with a smile. "Remember always I have the luck of the Irish." She was dress in her blue dress. "I can never hug you, but I can talk."

"Barney and John are going to dig up that leg," said Grandma. "And you're going to bug your father until he tells where it is buried." Then she disappeared with the elves.

Kitty saw her nightgown on the bed. She put it on and slipped into the cold bed. Only good thing was that the beautiful quilt that Grandma made for her was there. Kitty touched the year that Grandma sew it, 1874, for Kitty on her sixteen birthdays.

She loved Carl. Couldn't her father understand? Did he ever love Ann? She doubted it. Kitty yawned and was fast to sleep.

CHAPTER 4

+ + + + + +

Ms. Howard's Secret

C arl and Kitty decided to find flowers in the woods for Miss Howard. Their teacher had not been in school for weeks. Everyone in town was talking about her boyfriend, Roger Townsend. He was in the war, fighting. There was talk that he was dead.

"Do you think Miss Howard will let us visit her?" said Kitty.

"I have heard she doesn't see anyone," said Carl.

They didn't get to see each other often, especially alone. He moved over to her side. Kitty knew he was going to kiss her as soon as he was, she turned and ran down the path.

"Wait for me," yelled Carl. Then he heard a wagon coming; it was Dr. Smith.

"Where are you going?" asked Dr. Smith as pulled the two horses to a halt.

"We're gathered flowers for our teacher, Miss Howard," said Kitty.

"I'm going to pass right by the Howard's house. Would you two like a ride?"

"That would nice," said Carl. He helped Kitty into the small wagon.

"What is wrong with Miss Howard?" asked Kitty. She had been worried.

"If you two can keep a secret, there's good news coming for Miss Howard."

"What good news?" asked Kitty.

"It's not coming until Christmas, maybe Santa Claus will bring it," said Dr. Smith. "Here we are."

Miss Howard's brother asked who was at the door.

Carl knew him. "Hello, Peter, we are here to give flowers to Miss Howard."

"We miss her," said Kitty. She followed Peter into the house.

"Wait here," said Peter as he pointed to some chairs.

"I can't promise that she will come downstairs to see you, but I will try."

"So beautiful," Kitty said as admired everything in the room.

"I'm not into fancy things," said Carl.

Kitty saw Peter walk down the stairs. She quickly stood up when she saw Miss Howard walking slowly behind him. She was so thin and pale.

"Miss Howard, all the students miss you so much," said Kitty.

"Here's some flowers," said Carl. He handed them to Peter.

"It was nice of you to bring me flowers. I'm not your teacher now. Please call me, Rachel," she said as she pointed to the chairs.

"We will be good and study. Please come back to teach," said Kitty.

"I'll never walk in that school again." Then Rachel broke into sobs.

Kitty looked at Carl. "What did we do?"

"My dear, it's wasn't any of you." Rachel's face turned white. Her body began to start shaking with fear. She started to cry.

Kitty ran to her side. "Why are you so scared?" She hugged her.

"If I tell you"—she stood up and walk back and forth in the room—"can you keep a secret? I don't think anyone will believe me." She took out her handkerchief.

"Try us," said Carl. "We know lots of secrets we can't tell anyone."

"Please sit down, and I will tell you what happened. Three weeks ago, I stayed after school. I was working on a project. Suddenly, her face got pale, and she took a deep breath. I saw a tall, huge bear with big feet and sharp claws. I covered my nose with my hand because the smell was awful. He has long hair on his body. He came closer to me. I could see his eyes were dark black. And he had a flat nose. I was so scared.

"The monster walked up to my desk, and before I knew, I was in his arms. I had fainted. I woke up in a cave. I could hear a waterfall. I saw a family of bear. The mother of human bears came to look me over. She touched my hair. Then pick me up like a baby. I cried and cried. I want to go home. The next morning, the bear picked me up and took me back to the schoolhouse. I was thankful there was no school."

"Wow!" said Carl. "Thank God they didn't hurt you."

"I'll not go back to that school. He may come for me."

Kitty thought a minute, then walked around the large room. "Miss Howard, could you have school in this big room?"

"I would have to ask my father if that would be okay with him?"

A well-dressed man walked into the room. "My dear, I think would be perfect. Anything that would make you happy."

"Oh, Dad, I would love to see my students." She gave him a kiss on his check. He hugged her.

"When do you want to start? I'll can have the desks and chairs moved today."

"Dad, would you take Kitty and Carl home?"

"Your secret will be our secret," said Carl.

He followed Kitty out to Mr. Howard's buggy. His driver, Thomas, was waiting. When Thomas was near the forest, Carl said, "Thomas, you can stop here." Carl help Kitty down from the wagon. They followed the path until the came to the forest.

Kitty stopped at a sign, Keep Out. "Who craved these?"

Carl came near her. "I don't know." He pulled her nearer to kiss her. Kitty could feel his hands around her body.

"Let's get married. Then I could really show how much I love you."

Kitty pulled away. "I'm not ready to get married."

"Kitty, do you love me?" said Carl. "If you don't, I'll find another woman." Then he turned and walked down the path.

Kitty ran to him. "Carl, I love you, but please wait until we finish school."

Carl grabbed her and lifted her up to kiss her. "Promise me."

CHAPTER 5

✦ ✦✦✦✦ ✦

A Christmas to Remember

T he students were busy making decorations for the tree. They were excited because by their teacher, Miss Howard, told them she was going to ask their parents and siblings too. Everyone could help make this Christmas special.

A young man in an army uniform walked into the room. He had a missing leg. Ms. Howard ran into his arms with tears in her eyes.

"Will you marry me?" said Roger Townsend. He kissed her lips.

"Let's get married on Christmas Eve," said Rachel Howard.

Everyone clapped their hands. It was great to see their teacher happy.

"Let's go and tell my father," said Ms. Howard.

Little Sherry asked, "Who's going to be Baby Jesus?"

Miss Howard said, "I don't know."

"I'm sure my mother can spare a baby," said Carl with a grin.

Everyone laughed. They knew he had many siblings.

"I'm going into the deep forest to find a tall Christmas tree."

There was silence in the room, for everyone had been warned of the danger of going into the forest. Kitty said, "We can find one here."

"No," said Carl. "This huge room needs a tall tree." He looked at Billy. "Billy, will you go with me tomorrow?"

"I'm not going into that forest," said Billy. He shook his head.

Mr. Howard enter the room in time to hear Carl.

"You can use my wagon to bring the tree here," said Mr. Howard. He added, "The bears go to sleep during winter."

"Okay, I'll help you," said Billy.

"My driver will help you too," said Mr. Howard.

Snow was falling in the morning. Carl was waiting for Billy to come with Thomas, Mr. Howard's driver, and the wagon. He was cold waiting, but finally, he heard the horses coming.

Thomas was carrying a rife. "I'm not going in that forest without my gun."

"Let us go," said Carl. "We'll leave the wagon here."

Everyone heard a screaming. Carl could feel his body shiver.

"Let's hurry and do this," said Thomas. He had seen the bears with a human faces. A whole family of them lived near the waterfalls. "Carl, there's some big nice trees this way."

"Here's a tall tree," said Billy.

"Looks okay to me," said Thomas. He had experience cutting down big tree.

Carl glanced down the path they had come from. Quick as a flash, he saw brown fur flying by a tree.

"Let's get this tree out of here." Carl could feel his body shake.

Halfway down the trail to the wagon, they heard the loudest sound they had ever heard in their life. There in front of them was a giant of a bear with a human face. His nose was flat with dark black eyes and long waving brown hair.

Billy was so scared. He cried. "Thomas shoot him."

"Do not run," said Thomas. "If you run, he will chase you."

Carl thought of the jerky in his pocket. He pulled out a piece and threw it in front of the bear. The bear grabbed it and ran away.

"Let's not tell anyone that we saw a big bear," said Carl. He thought one more secret not to tell anyone.

It was Christmas Eve; the tree was decorated beautifully. The parents and friends were coming in the door. Mr. Howard greeted everyone with a Merry Christmas.

"Who's playing Santa Claus?" asked Kitty.

"You will find out," said Carl.

"Are you keeping a secret from me?

"Kitty," said Sarah, "Miss Howard wants you to come to her bedroom."

Kitty walked up the many steps. She heard Miss Howard's voice. The door was opened. Kitty walked inside to see Ms. Howard.

"You're beautiful."

"Thanks, I want you to be my bridesmaid."

"Oh, I can't." Kitty looked down at her dress.

"Your dress is hanging up in my closet." Rachel walked over and carried the blue dress to Kitty. "It's your gift from me. If it wasn't for Carl and you to help me...Please put it on."

Kitty never touched a fabric so soft and pretty.

"Let me fix your hair up to night."

"Look in the mirror—wait, I forget something." Rachel opened a black case. "Here, you can have this too."

"Oh, it's beautiful," said Kitty with tears in eyes. "You are so good to me."

"Here, let me put this neckline on your neck."

Kitty gave Rachel a hug. "Thank you."

There was a knock on the door. "Rachel, it's time," said Peter.

Peter and Carl were waiting with Roger and Pastor Bell. Kitty smiled at Carl. Carl wanted to grab her and kiss her. Mr. Howard took his daughter's arm, and they walked slowly over to them. Rachel kissed her father. She walked to Roger's side. Roger was handsome too. He said yes. And Rachel said yes.

Mr. Howard kissed his daughter on her check and shook his hands with his new son-in-law. "Congratulation's to a lovely couple."

Then Mr. Howard said, "Now let's have the Christmas play."

All the students sang, "Away in the Manger," as Mary and Joseph walked slowly to the Baby Jesus in the wooden crib. Carl could look out the big window from his chair. He got a little nervous in his seat when he saw a huge bear. He walked over to Thomas.

"Do not worry," Thomas said. "They come here often. I have seen the bears sit by the window outside, listening to Rachel sing and play the piano. They seem loved to hear the music."

"Ho, ho, ho, Merry Christmas," said a loud voice.

Everyone was excited and said, "Merry Christmas, Santa Claus."

Santa pulled out a gift. "The first gift is for Kitty." He walked over to Kitty and gave her a gift.

"Thanks! Santa."

"Everyone gets a candy cane and a book," said Mr. Howard.

Kitty was sitting in the wagon, waiting for her father to come. He was talking to Mr. Howard. She heard a loud screaming sound. Chills ran down her spine.

"Papa, please hurry." Kitty jumped with fear when someone touched her arm. She came face-to-face with a bear. He had the dark eyes and a flat nose. And he smelled so bad that she fainted. The bear took off when he saw a man coming toward him.

Bob thought Kitty was sleeping, so he covered her up with a blanket. He told the horses to hurry home. Bob was glad there was a full moon.

CHAPTER 6

◆◆◆◆◆

A Hurried-Up Wedding

B ob told Kitty that he wanted to talk to her after supper. Kitty wondered why he was so serious, and they ate in silence. She washed and dried the dishes, then went out to the porch. Her father was sitting in his chair, smoking his pipe. Kitty waited until he spoke. She twisted her fingers.

"The whole town is talking about you," Bob said without glancing at her. "It's what you and Carl did."

"What did we do?" asked Kitty. Her blue eyes widen.

"That you two are fooling around and kissing in public." He turned his eyes toward hers. "You are embarrassing us. I should have told you about this young man's thoughts." Bob looked up to see Ann walking toward Kitty. He wished she would stay out of this, but he knew she wouldn't.

Ann's brown eyes stared at Kitty. She didn't want Kitty to make the same mistakes she had made with men. "Is that what you want to be? A bad girl?" said Ann, then she heard the horses and wagon coming into the yard.

"That's Carl's folks." She looked at Bob. "Go and let them in, we will come to the living room in a minute."

"Why is Carl's parents here?" asked Kitty. She wished she had cleaned up a little. She wondered if Carl was with them.

"I went to town to get some coffee," said Ann, "And what did I hear?" Ann pointed her finger in Kitty's face. "You have been fooling around with Carl." She grabbed Kitty's arm roughly. "Let's have a talk with Carl's parents."

Kitty was so humiliated when she walked into the living room with her mother pulling her along as if she was a toddler in trouble. She held back her tears. She couldn't look at Rose and Carl Senior in their faces. And Carl had a grin on his face!

She was not happy. Her father was speaking, so she turned her eyes toward him.

"I have talked to the Pastor Bell. He agrees with me, the sooner that these young folks get married, the better it will be for every-one." He cleared his throat. "The pastor will not marry them in the church. He will marry them this Sunday after church in his office."

Rose and Carl Senior nodded their heads. "We'll be there,"'

They glanced at their son. They couldn't believe that Pastor Bell would be so unkind and not let them have a wedding in the church. After all, their son wasn't the only young man who got his sweetheart in trouble. Rose knew they did.

Carl was glad to marry Kitty. He was in love with Kitty. Yesterday, he went to town to get groceries for his mother. Bob Kelly was in the store. Bob said he was glad Carl was marrying Kitty. He was giving them the forest and the old cabin.

Bob was thrilled someday; he could have a sawmill. There was plenty of wood even to build a nice house. Kitty was the only girl he loved.

"Kitty, did you kiss Carl?" asked Ann with her hands on her hips. "Did you two fool around with each other?"

Kitty had tears in her eyes. She couldn't talk.

"Ann," said Bob. "I think they will make a nice couple." He looked over at Rose. She helped delivered his daughter. Bob knew that she would be kind to Kitty.

"They sure will be a lovely couple," said Rose with a smile.

"Great," said Ann in a rough voice, "Then my daughter will not be a bad girl."

"Kitty and I have not done anything wrong," said Carl. "You have no right to think that." He walked over to Kitty. "Kitty, I love you and will be happy to have you as my wife." He took her hand in his and kiss it.

Kitty's tears ran down her face. She didn't want to get married now. She liked Carl very much, but not to be his wife.

"I do not want to get married," Kitty said as she dropped Carl's hand. She ran upstairs to her room, sobbing.

"Why did Ann call me a bad girl?" Kitty said out loud. She didn't see Grandma sitting in her favorite chair.

"You're not," said Grandma. "Ann is unkind to you. I wish I told my son years ago to take her back to Alaska."

"I want to finish school," said Kitty. "I don't want to get married and have babies." She looked up, and her Grandma was gone.

CHAPTER 7

Kitty's Wedding Day

Kitty was awaked by her mother's voice. "Get up, lazy bones." Ann grabbed the white dress that she had made for Kitty. "Wear this dress." She hurried to the bedroom door. "I must get ready."

Rachel had given her a beautiful dress and a necklace, but her mother made her give it back to Rachel. Ann told Rachel that Kitty has no need for fancy clothes. Her eyes were red from crying; she was being forced to marry Carl.

Kitty told her father she was too young to get married. He said most of the girls are married at sixteen.

Kitty tried to put her hair up like Rachel did, but it didn't look good. She let her long red hair hang down to her waist.

"Kitty," said her father, "it's time to go to the church."

Kitty wanted to run away, instead she walked down the steps slowly. She walked outside to where Bob and Ann were waiting for her.

Bob helped her up to the wagon seat. He knew Kitty was upset. He whispered, "This is for your own good."

Kitty didn't answer when he asked her if she loved Carl. At this moment, she hated him, but in her heart, she did love him. Carl and his parents and all his siblings were waiting for them. Carl smiled at Kitty. He was walking toward her, carrying flowers. Kitty picked up her long dress to walk.

Carl said, "I know you don't want to be marry now, but I can't wait any longer because I love you."

Kitty had tears in her light-blue eyes. Carl reached down to kiss her.

"I'm not pretty." She showed him how big the dress was.

"I'd told you before, I didn't care for all those fancy things," said Carl.

Then he took her hand in his. They walked over to where Pastor Bell was saying, "There's too many here for my small office, so we will have to go inside the church."

Pastor Bell said, "Will you, Carl, marry Kitty."

Carl smiled and said yes.

Then he looked at Kitty's sad face. "And you, Kitty, will marry Carl?"

Kitty whispered yes.

"Good," said Pastor Bell, "You're married, now come to my office and let's sign those papers."

Outside the church, Carl took Kitty in his arms and kiss her lips. She kissed him back. Carl said, "I wished we had a pretty wedding like Rachel. But we are lucky to have each other." He kissed her again.

"I don't have all day," said Pastor Bell. "You two can do that later."

There was no cake, no fancy food, or any town folks to celebrate the wedding. She didn't even have a ring or a pretty dress.

Bob was telling Carl and Kitty that his mother wanted Kitty to have all her pretty dishes and the furniture. "I'll bring it over this afternoon."

Rose gave Kitty a nice hug. "I'm happy to have you as a daughter." She gave Kitty a bag of food. "I'll see you soon. We have a cow, chickens, and a hog. We'll bring them over soon."

Kitty didn't want to live so close to the woods, but Carl was thrilled to know he would own the forest for the wood. "I'll get a sawmill and build a larger cabin for our children." Kitty wished he would just shut up.

Carl's parents and siblings had when to the cabin to clean.

"The barn looks good for as old as it is." Carl helped Kitty down from the wagon. "I'll have to take care of the horses."

Kitty walked to the log cabin. This was where her great-grand-parents lived and raised their three children. There was a table in the kitchen with a few chairs. The bedroom had a wooden bed. She put the food on the table that Rose had given her. There was coffee, jar of jam, a loaf of fresh bread, bacon, and eggs.

Ann would only let her wash and dry dishes. She didn't know how to cook or bake bread. She had a lot to learn.

Carl came in with a pile of wood for the little stove. "We will have coffee soon." They ate some bread and blueberry jam. "Bob will be here with your grandma's furniture. That will make this place looks nice. The curtains are bad, but you can sew some new ones."

Sew, thought Kitty. *I must sew. I'm not going to like marriage life.* She stared at the wooden floor, wishing she wasn't here.

"Carl, what are those red marks on the wood? Does it look like blood?"

"If it's blood, it's not my relatives. Must be yours?"

CHAPTER 8

－◆◆◆◆◆－

Kitty Is Sick

K itty was sick. She had thrown up several times. "Carl, I've been sick. I don't want you to bother me with your thing."

"It's not a thing," said Carl. He started to laugh. "It's a baby machine maker. My father made ten babies with his thing."

"I'm too young to have a baby," said Kitty. "Besides, I don't want one."

Carl reached for her body. He loved the color of her red hair. He pulled a curl.

"We'll not have one," said Kitty. "I'm not going to have a baby every year." She pulled away. "My mother only had one. That was me."

"That's because she died having you," said Carl as he reached for her again.

"How do you know that?"

"Everyone in town knows," said Carl. He pulled up her night-gown slowly.

"My mother delivered you."

Kelly moved his hand away. She sat up in bed. "Your mother!"

Carl pulled her down in bed. "Now I'm going to use my 'thing' and make you a baby. Do you want a girl or a boy?"

Kitty didn't have a chance to say anything. Even if she was sick, he was unkind to her. She couldn't sleep thinking why her father didn't tell her that Ann wasn't her mother. And who was Ann? Was her mother buried in that cemetery behind the house? Or in the grave craved into the cross *I was murdered?*

She slipped back to bed not to awake her husband. Sleep just wouldn't come. Carl jumped out of bed to put more wood on the stove. He glanced out the window.

"Kitty, it's snowing!" He yelled from the kitchen.

Kitty didn't answer. She buried her head under Grandma's quilt. Suddenly the quilt was pulled off her body. Carl wrapped the quilt around his body.

"It's snowing!" He gave her a kiss. "Time to make babies."

Kitty said, "I have to go to the potty."

"I'll be here waiting," said Carl. He lay down on the bed. "My 'thing' can wait too."

Kitty turned back to the bedroom. "I need to talk to my father." She pulled her work dress over her head. She didn't even brush her hair. Kitty went to the kitchen to start Carl's breakfast.

"Well, it's snowing pretty good," said Carl. "Perhaps tomorrow, I will take you to your father since you're a spoiled Daddy's girl."

"I'm not," said Kitty. "You're the mean one." She threw a towel at him.

"I'm the mean one?" said Carl with a loud voice. "I better feed the animals before I get mad."

"You don't need a baby because you are one."

He reached for his jacket and slammed the door. Kitty started to sob. Suddenly two elves appeared. She yelled at them to go to bed.

Carl came inside the cabin. He was carrying firewood. "Boy, it's cold outside." He grinned as he poured himself some coffee. "I can't work outside, so I will have to work on making babies."

Kitty's Irish temper got the best of her. She picked up her cup of coffee and threw it at him. "I wish I never married you."

Carl caught the cup. "Breaking your grandmother's Irish cups. She's going to be mad. Besides it wouldn't' make any different who you married. Any young stud like me is going to enjoy making babies. That is part of married life. Grow up. Someday you'll be begging for a poke." He grabbed his jacket and went back to the barn.

Kitty cried. "I'll never beg for one."

"Yes, you will." Grandma Kitty Ann laughed. She was sitting in the chair next to her.

"He wants six babies!" Kitty sobbed. "I'm the one who has to have them."

"That's your job," said Grandma. "You're to please your husband."

"Please him?" said Kitty. "What about me?"

"When your baby is born in September, you'll be so proud and happy."

"I wish my father didn't push me into getting married."

Grandma was getting ready to leave.

"Don't go. I want to ask who my mother was. Carl told me that my mother died having me."

"You better ask your father."

"Who Ann is too?"

"By the way, asked him where the leg is. He may tell you," said Grandma as disappeared.

Kitty glanced out the window. Carl was coming to the door with more firewood. She opened the door for him.

Carl took off his jacket. He grinned. "Are you ready for a poke?"

Kitty couldn't help herself. He looked so handsome with that dimple on his check. She knew down in her heart that she loved him. She ran into his arms.

Carl picked her up and carry his bride to their bedroom. "This time, it will not be dark, and I will see everything." He grinned. "Kitty, you know I love you since we were young. It was better we married early because I'm madly in love with you."

Kitty unbuttoned his shirt. She knew that Carl loved her. She knew now that marriage is more than making babies. It's knowing what really love is. "I love you, Carl."

CHAPTER 9

$\bullet\spadesuit\spadesuit\spadesuit\spadesuit\bullet$

Rose Has a Secret Too

"You sure are getting big," said Carl's mother, Rose. She touched Kitty's stomach. "I bet you're going have twins."

"I hope not," said Kitty. "I don't think I can take care of one."

"Have you seen Ann lately?" asked Rose. She sat down beside Kitty to nurse her new baby.

"I hope I don't have to do that," Kitty asked. "How many times a day?"

Rose laughed. "Babies are hungry."

"I saw Ann at Christmas. She didn't even talk to me."

Kitty had talked to her father about her mother, but he refused to talk about her. She even asked him who was buried it the grave marked, I WAS MURDERED. Her father told her that it was none of her business.

"It's her heart," said Rose. "She asked about you."

Kitty didn't say anything. Carl and his father walked inside the house. She was thinking about Ann. Why she didn't like her.

Carl said something to Kitty, but she was in deep in thought. He touched her arm. "Kitty, are you okay?"

"Yes, I was just thinking," said Kitty.

"What about?" asked Carl as reached down to kiss her lips.

"About my mother."

"My mother knew Carolina well since the first grade."

"Really?" said Kitty her eyes widen. "The first grade?"

Rose had come back from putting her baby down to sleep.

"I'm going to the barn," said Carl. He looked at his mother. "It's time to tell Kitty the secrets that you know about her mother."

"Do you think it's a good time in her condition?"

"Yes, Mom, I do," said Carl. He walked out of the house.

"Please, tell me about my mother."

Rose didn't want to remember what happen to Carolina, but it was time that Kitty knew the truth. She took a deep breath. "We went to school together, got married about the same time too. Her parents were from the town of Seattle. Her father was a banker here in Howard Town." She took her handkerchief out of her apron pocket. Rose knew she was going to cry. It so awful what happened.

"Carolina loved your father. She was so happy when she learned she was with child. Her parents wanted to take her to live with relatives in Seattle. They were going to take her away and keep the baby a secret. Carolina ran off with Bob to the cabin in woods." Rose stopped talking. She knew this part was going to be hard to tell. She loved Carolina. Rose couldn't control her tears.

"Bob went to town to buy supplies." Rose started sobbing. "Carolina was still alive when Bob came home, but she was in labor. Bob rode his horse as fast as he could to our house. He helped me onto his horse. Bob told me on the way that four Indians came to the cabin and raped her. I couldn't believe what I saw when I opened the door.

"The Indian had scalped her. Blood was running down her face. They cut off her tits. Her blood was all over the room." Rose stopped to catch her breath. Her tears were rolling down her checks. "Carolina told us what happened. She screamed in labor pain. She said to me, 'Rose, please save my baby, just save her, don't worry about me.' Carolina gashed for air to breathe. I looked down and saw the baby's head. I told Carolina to push hard, and her baby girl was born. Carolina hugged her baby with blood running down her face and tears flowing down her checks. 'Bob, please kiss our baby goodnight,' said Carolina. 'That kiss will be from me.'

"Bob was sobbing when she closed her blue eyes." Rose wiped her tears. "She was in awful pain. I was glad she died because now she was in peace."

Rose and Kitty were both crying. Rose held Kitty in her arms tight. "Your mother loved you." She wiped her tears. "We sure could use a good cup of tea." Rose got up from her chair to make the tea.

Kitty slipped on her tea. "Please tell me more."

"Your father grabbed his rife and ran out of the door. He was yelling, 'I will kill them.' He was like a madman. Bob was gone for six months. Kitty, I have a secret," said Rose. She touched Kitty's hand. "I lied to Carolina's parents. I told them her baby had die too. I had to lie. If Bob came home and knew I gave them his daughter—" Rose started to cry again. She had another secret but didn't dare tell Kitty. "Carolina told me not to tell Bob."

"I have many secrets," said Kitty. "I'm glad you lied."

"When Bob came back home with Ann, his hair had turned gray, and he looked older. For days, he never said a word. At night, he went out to bury something. One day, when you were smiling, I told Bob to hold his daughter. He sobbed and sobbed. 'She looks like her mother.' Carolina wanted you to kiss her goodnight, so you better start tonight."

Kitty dried her tears. "Thanks, I know it was hard to tell me, but I am glad you did."

It was a beautiful day. Kitty was sitting outside in a chair on the porch that Carl had made. She told him it wouldn't be long for this baby to be born.

He laughed and said, "Twins."

That night, her labor started. She screamed in pain. Carl got dressed. He went to get his mother.

Rose checked Kitty over, then said to Carl, "You better go to town and get Dr. Smith."

"Dr. Smith!" said Carl. His mother whispered something to her son's ear.

"What wrong?" Kitty asked in between her labor pain.

"It is just that I have never delivery twins before."

Carl gave Kitty a kiss. "I'll be right back."

Dr. Smith walked in door. He looked at Kitty. "Twins for sure. Rose, you're right. One twin is coming the wrong the way, but the first baby is coming headfirst. That's good. How old are you, Kitty?" asked the doctor.

"I'm seventeen," said Kitty said. She was scared. Was she was going to die like her mother?

The pain was so bad. Kitty said to Carl, "I am never going to do this again." She screamed, "Never."

"You better find some brandy," said Dr. Smith.

"Carl, give some to your wife and then take the rest of the bottle to the barn. And stay there until I call you."

Carl kissed Kitty and told her he loved her. Then he and walked slowly to the barn, carrying his bottle of brandy.

Kitty's first baby was a boy; he was crying. Second baby was a girl. She was very small and weak. He put out a small baby bottle out of his black bag, told Rose to use it to feed the baby a little warm coffee at a time, every two hours, and wrap her in a warm blanket.

"Coffee!" said Rose. "Awful young to drink coffee."

"It works good for her heart." Dr. Smith closed his black bag with a bang. He told Rose that Kitty should stay in bed until I tell her to get up. She can use the potty.

"Rose, if she starts bleeding heavy, sent Carl to get me." Dr. Smith opened the door. "I am going out to the barn to talk to Carl to tell he is a proud father of twins."

In the barn, Carl and Dr. Smith sat down on a wooden bench and finished the rest of the brandy.

"Kitty and twins are lucky to be alive," said Dr. Smith.

"Thanks to God and you," said Carl.

Carl kissed his wife and said, 'Thanks for the twins. We have one of each now. What shall we name them?"

"We shall call the girl, Kathleen," said Kitty Ann as she kissed her daughter's forehead. "That's from my mother and Robert."

Many town folks came over to see the twins, bringing gifts too.

One Sunday, the pastor came to bless the babies. Robert let out a cry, but Kathleen ran a high fever. Dr. Smith came to the house. He shook his head when he looked at the wee baby.

That night, Kathleen died. Kitty sobbed and sobbed. Carl spent his time in the barn, building a wooden coffin box. Tears ran down his checks as pounded some nails. Then he rode to town and came back with a gift for Kitty. Kitty was surprised to find a beautiful blue dress. Carl carried his son, Robert, and held Kitty's right hand tight. They both tried to hold back their tears, but it hurt so much inside that their tears ran down.

CHAPTER 10

————— ✦✦✦✦✦ —————

Ann's Secrets

Kitty asked Carl if he would take care of Robert; she wanted to walk over to see her father and Ann.

"No problem," said Carl. "I heard that Ann isn't well."

"I will be back in a few hours." Kitty kissed Carl.

It had been awhile since she walked over to her father's house. Kitty saw her father sitting in a chair on the front porch, smoking his pipe. She waved to him.

"Good to see you, Kitty." Bob stood up and hugged his daughter. He kissed her forehead. Kitty smiled.

"How is Ann today?" She sat down in the other chair.

"She is sleeping. It's her heart. Dr. Smith was here. He said she didn't have long to live."

"I am sorry to hear that," said Kitty. "Does she have any relatives?"

"No, her parents died years ago."

"How did you meet Ann?"

"When I went to Alaska." He pulled on his beard with his hand. He was nervous. Bob didn't want to talk.

"Dad, I know how my real mother died?"

"Who told you? I thought it was a secret." Bob rubbed his hands together. "Did she tell you everything?"

Kitty look down at her dusty boots. "Rose loved Carolina."

"That is true. She took care of you for a while."

Bob got up from his chair and said, "So you know now that Ann is not your mother?"

Kitty nodded her head. "Why didn't you tell me? Why did you keep it a secret?"

Bob glanced away from her eyes. "You needed a mother. I needed someone. After your mother died, I went to find those rotten Indians. I wanted to kill them, but I never found them. I spent my time drinking every night. I would cry myself to sleep. I loved your mother so much. Awful way to die. I had dreams of seeing her with her forehead scalp and her tits cut off and all that blood. I hope those four Indians go to hell. They raped her." Bob had tears in his eyes, then he sobbed. His body shook.

Kitty got up to hug him. Her eyes were full of tears.

He sat down on his rocker. "I met Ann as a hooker. We drank until we passed out. One day, I told her what happened to my wife, and that the baby was alive. I had a daughter. I was done with drinking that day. I wanted to go back home and take care of my daughter. Ann told me she would come with me and help take of her. She didn't have any place to go too. I didn't have any money to get back to Washington. She pulled out a box full of money.

"One night, we went back to mother's house. She wasn't happy about Ann, and I never married. She got mad. Ann had you call her mother. I didn't love her." Bob put his head down. "I don't think she was ever loved because she didn't know how to love someone. She was thirteen when she became a bad girl. Only way to live was to spread her legs. Ann had a hard life. She had no love inside to give to others."

Kitty understood why she was so cold and unhappy. Her heart was sad for Ann. "Dad, do you think I can see her?"

"I don't know." Bob stood up. "She doesn't want see people. I will go and see if she is sleeping. Dr. Smith told she hasn't long to live." He walked away. He had some feelings for Ann, but his heart was still in love with Carolina and will be forever. He couldn't marry another woman.

Kitty sat and waited. Kitty didn't know what she was going to say to her mother who wasn't her mother.

Her father called Kitty to come inside, "Ann is in her room."

Kitty had never been in Ann's room. She walked slowly up the stair passed Grandma's room to Ann's. The door was open. Kitty didn't know what to say, and it just came out, "Mom?"

Ann smiled, and then she cried. She dried her tears with her handkerchief. "Come sit beside the bed."

Kitty said, "I am sorry to hear you been sick."

Ann replied, "I am sorry about Kathleen. I had a little girl. I called her Bonnie. She was beautiful. My husband and Bonnie died from high fever. After they all died, I had to go to work. I was a whore. Your father took me away from there. I knew he didn't love me." Ann started coughing. Kitty reached for her water glass. "I'm sorry I wasn't kind to you. I am glad you came to see me," said Ann. She took a deep breath. "Look in that top drawer. Some men didn't have dollars to buy for a poke. They gave me gold, watches, and rings.

"I want you to have what's in the drawer, some gold from gold mine. Wrap all up in that towel and keep it. Your husband wants a sawmill. You can buy it for him. Come near, Kitty, call me mom, tell me you love me. Please don't tell my secret of the man who was murdered. I asked God to forgive me."

Kitty told Ann she loved her. Ann closed her eyes. Kitty walked down the steps. Her father was outside, smoking his pipe. "You sure were there a long time."

"Papa, Ann is dead." She sobbed in his arms.

CHAPTER 11

Ann's Funeral

"Ann requested a very private funeral," said Bob as he put down her letter. She also wrote that she wanted to be buried next to the grave, I WAS MURDERED.

"What?" said Carl. He glanced over to Kitty. "We are not going to have a cemetery for everyone."

Bob stood up from his chair. He walked back and forth. "She'll never know where she's buried. I'll bury her in my backyard."

"Time for bed," said Carl. He picked up his son and hugged him.

"Say good night to your grandfather," said Kitty.

Bob was telling Kitty, "We will have to bury her tomorrow."

Carl came back and poured some coffee. "More, Bob?"

Bob shook his head. "I better go home before it gets to dark."

Kitty stood up to her five feet height. "Dad, Ann can be buried in the backyard. But first, I want to know who is buried in that grave and who killed him. When I talked to her before she died, she said, 'I asked God to forget me.'"

Kitty told her father starting at the beginning.

Bob cleared his voice. "Ann paid my way back to Seattle area. She wanted to come and help take care of Kitty. She didn't have a place to go. Ann got the tickets, and when we came aboard the ship, she said, 'Oh by the way, I took along my daughter and husband too.' I was surprised. Then she said, 'Don't worry, they're dead.' When we arrived at the port, she brought a wagon and horses to carry the coffins.

"Ann told me that her husband died because of yellow fever. On the boat, she told me that he was a gambler, and one night, he was found cheating, and a miner shot him."

"Did the baby died from a high fever?" asked Kitty.

"She said so," said Bob, "but she lied so many times."

"Why did Ann asked God to forgive her?" said Kitty.

Bob stood up. "I need some fresh air."

Kitty followed him outside. "Dad!"

Bob turned around and looked at his daughter.

"What was her secret? Did she kill her husband?"

Bob closed his eyes a minute. "I don't know."

Then he said, "That's a secret we will never know."

He gave his daughter a kiss on her forehead. "Thanks."

Carl walked outside. "Bob, I'll bring our wagon over to help you with Ann's body. He walked to the barn to make a wooden coffin."

Early in the morning, before Kitty got up, Carl had gone to help Bob. When she was feeding Robert his breakfast, she heard the wagon stopping in the backyard.

"I think we dug enough," said Bob. "I need a drink of some water."

"Kitty will have lunch ready." Carl sat down on the grass.

"I'm not hungry," said Bob. He yawned. He couldn't sleep last night. He was wondering who craved, I WAS MURDERED.

"Grandpa and Daddy, Mom told me to tell you to come," Robert said.

Carl jumped up when it came to eat. He was always ready.

"I'm going to put on my best dress," said Kitty. She got up from the table.

Bob said, "I'll be glad when this day is over."

"I have a sign to make," said Carl. He got up and went to the barn. "Robert, you and I are going to the edge of the forest to find some wildflowers."

"Look, they're plenty of flowers, daisy and buttercups." Kitty's so busy that she didn't see her son walked farther into the woods.

When she looked up, she couldn't see him anywhere. Kitty screamed her son's name. "Robert!"

He came running to her. "I told you before never go into that forest."

"It is not dark, Mommy, you said when it's dark, don't go in."

"There's brown bears that will eat you up."

Robert eyes were big. "Eat me?" Then he cried.

Kitty hugged her son. "Promise me, you will never go in that forest. We better go home."

"Kitty, you have your Bible. We will say the Lord's Prayer," said Bob.

Kitty and Robert put flowers on Ann's grave. Carl had put her name on the wooden cross.

"I don't ever know her last name," said Bob. "She never told me."

CHAPTER 12

+ ♦ ♦♦♦ ♦ +

Bob's Secret

Bob couldn't sleep. He tossed and turned. Finally, he got up from his bed and got dressed. He went outside to sit in his chair. It was lonely living alone, but his dreams were keeping him from sleeping. He was chasing the Indians who killed Kitty's mother. He woke up crying. Bob was sick of keeping secrets. He was ten when his great-grandfathers told him a secret where Bigfoot's leg was buried.

And that was only one secret. The secret that bother him the most was the secret of who Kitty's father was. *Would she still love me? I have been her father in name since she was born. I love her with all my heart. I want to carry that secret with me to my coffin.*

"How can I die in peace?" said Bob. "That I am not her father. I married her mother because I loved her. When Carolina told me that she was carrying a baby and her parents wanted to give it away, she begged me to marry her. I told I loved her. I still do."

Early in the morning, Bob rode over to the old cabin to talk to Kitty. He didn't want too, but the truth must be told. *Should I tell her all my secrets? No wonder my heart is giving out. It's too much stress.*

"Good morning, Grandpa," said Robert. He was now ten years old. He was imaged of his father with his waving brown hair.

"Good morning, Dad," Kitty said as she helped little Carl Junior get dressed.

Bob gave her and the children all hugs.

"What's up?" Kitty asked her father as she gave her son some wooden horses that Carl had made for him.

Bob twisted his long fingers. He rubbed his white beard. This wasn't going to be easy. "I had to keep my secrets."

"Oh, what secret was that?" asked Kitty.

"Where Bigfoot's leg is buried."

"All this time you knew where the leg was?"

"I was to keep it a secret from my grandmother. I kept the secret that Ann wasn't your mother until Rose told you the truth." Bob had tears in his blue eyes. "I still have dreams about what the Indians did to Carolina."

Kitty handed him her handkerchief.

He hold a deep breath. "I knew my mother kept two elves in her wooden chest that her mother brought from Northern Ireland."

Kitty knew also that Grandma was an Irish ghost. Her father was acting like he was on his deathbed. "I kept the secret that Ann murdered her husband. When I was very drunk one night in Alaska, I told her my secrets. Then she told me hers. One secret I never told her was—" Bob stood up. He looked out the window. He couldn't control his emotions; he sobbed. "I hope you will forgive me."

"Forgive you, Dad?" Kitty got up to touch his forehead with her hand. "Are you sick?"

"I kept the secret that Carolina was with child before we were married. She went that summer to visit her grandparents in Seattle. A handsome man, she told me, won her emotions. She said she never saw him again. Her parents knew it when she had morning sickness. They wanted to give the baby away. Carolina came to me crying. I had always loved her. We went to Pastor Bell. He married us, and we went to live in this cabin."

Bob sobbed. "Carolina was your mother, but I am not your father. I loved you since I first saw you. I'm sorry." He hung his head, and his tears fall. "Kitty, I couldn't tell you the truth." He sobbed. "I wanted you to love me."

Kitty got up from her chair and hugged him.

"You knew that Ann would tell if you didn't do what she said. You're the only father I have." She kissed him. He hugged her tight. "I will always call you dad, and I love you."

That night, she told Carl she was going to bed early. Kitty opened her bedroom door and saw two elves on her pillow. And her Grandma was sitting in her chair. "You better ask Rose for the truth. Bob doesn't know the truth."

Kitty gathered up her friends.

"Did you tell her where the gold is?" said Barney. "Let's go. Kitty is tired."

"Wait, Grandma," said Kitty. "What secret does Rose knows?"

Grandma again disappeared. She wished that she would go with her elves too and go back to Ireland.

CHAPTER 13

————— ◆◆◆◆◆ —————

Great-Grandma's Letter, Dated 1859

K itty heard her grandmother calling her to come to the bedroom. She went into the room to see Grandma sitting on the bed with her two little friends.

"I opened the chest. I wanted you to read this letter my mother wants you to know about her life." Grandma handed Kitty a brown with Celtic letters.

Kitty said, "I can't read this."

"That's why I am here," said Kitty Ann. She took the letter from Kitty. Grandma hold it over her heart. "My sweet dear, Mommy."

Kitty sat down in a chair to listen to her great-grandma's story.

Grandma cleared her throat again. "This is my story that I want my children to know and their children. My father wanted to go to the New Land to across the ocean. We lived in Illinois until my father decided to pack us up to move to this forest. The Seattle Indians were friendly. They helped us how to build this log cabin. The chief told us about the big bears that lived in this forest before they came to live in Washington. We call them Bigfoot because they have feet like a giant. Perhaps in one time, they were giants. They stand up right and walk. Nature cover their bodies with hair so they were warm. They want to live alone. Great-grandma wants to tell you this story. They were living in the log cabin. My husband, William, had gone to town to buy supplies. I was called Kitty Ann after my mother. I was alone in the cabin, washing the kitchen floor, when I heard a screaming sound, and suddenly the door came open, and a tall bear bent his head down so he could come inside.

"I never was so scared when I saw his long dirty claws. When he moved toward me, his long brown hair was flying. I wanted to scream, but no sounds came out. Then I saw his leg. He had been shot. The blood was pouring out of his leg. His dark eyes were begging me to help him.

"My father in Northern Ireland was a doctor. I had worked with him for many years. I knew what I had to do. He was awful pain. He made crying sounds. Then he collapsed in the middle of the kitchen. I knew that William's homemade blackberries would put him to sleep. I went into the bedroom to get my father's medicine bag. He had insisted that we take it. I found William's wine. I took both jugs to the bear. He drank all of it. It didn't take long for him to go to sleep. I heard William's wagon come into the yard. I ran outside to tell him we had a bear in our kitchen.

"He said, 'What?' William ran to get his rifle out of the wagon. 'No, William, he is hurt. Someone shot him in his leg.' 'I don't care. I'll shoot him right in his heart.' 'No, William, you go to the barn and bring the saw to the house.' 'Why?' said William. 'The saw?' 'Because you're going to cut off his leg?' 'I'm going to kill him before I do that.' 'Please, honey, help me cut off his leg, if you won't, he will die.' 'He could turn on us and kill us.' 'I gave two jugs of your wine, and when we start, I'll give him a shot for him to stay asleep.' 'You gave him my good wine!'

"It took a long time to cut off his leg. William would cut, then I would stitch. It was thru the bone. It was getting dark. I held lantern up for him to see. I keep praying to God he would stay asleep. I was on my knees washing up all the blood. It smelled awful. I found a mask in Dad's bag. I told William to go to washhouse to clean up. He was covered with blood.

"'What do you want me to do with his leg?' 'I'll help you carry it to the barn. We will cover it now with hay, and later you can buried it. We must keep this secret.' I went to the washhouse. I was sick to my stomach. I was carrying my first child. I hadn't told my husband. I was glad the bear was sleeping when I gave him a double shot of sleeping medicine. It worked great because he slept four days. He was healing so fast. William made him a wooden cane and showed him how to walk with it. I was surprised when he called me Kitty. He bent his head down like he was bowing to me, his way of saying thanks. That was the day when he walked back to the deep forest.

"William told me to wipe my tears, 'Your baby has gone home.' I told him no my baby was in my stomach. William was so happy. Many times, we have found big leaves with all kinds of berries. We know that Bigfoot brought it because there was only one big footprint in the dirt.

"What I wish to tell you that Bigfoot bears chase you out of their forests because they want to live in peace. I asked William where he had buried the leg. He told no one will find it."

CHAPTER 14

✦ ✦✦✦✦ ✦

Robert Is Lost

"**C**arl," said Kitty, "where is Robert?" She saw him when she was hanging out the clothes on the line.

"He is probably playing hide-and-seek. You know how he loves hid from us. I'll look in the barn."

Kitty told Carl. She was going into the cabin to look under his bed. Kitty went outside to shout, "Robert, we are having cookies."

When he didn't come, she was scared. She ran into cabin. "He is gone."

Carl looked at his wife's worried face. "He wouldn't go in the forest, would he?"

"I hope not. We told him many times not to go there," said Kitty as she sat down.

"I'll go look for him before it gets dark." Carl picked up his rifle. "Don't worry, we will find him."

Kitty watched him go into the forest when she turned around to see her Grandma's elves.

"We are going to look for Robert," said the elves in the same breath.

"You both are two little," said Kitty, "you'll be lost too." They were gone before Kitty finished talking.

"Lord, please bring Carl and Robert home." Kitty thought of something her father told her that the big bears lived near a waterfall.

"Molly, I want you to take care of Carl Junior," said Kitty as she put the shawl. "I know where Robert is hiding. I will go and find him."

"And Daddy too?" said Molly. She had tears in her eyes.

Kitty turned around to see her grandma sitting in a chair.

"My little folks told me Kitty needs some help."

"Molly, this is my grandma. She will stay here until I come back."

"Take a lantern with you," said Grandma.

Kitty grabbed matches and the lantern. "Pray that I will find them."

When she got to the edge of forest, a chill ran down her spine, but her love for Carl and Robin gave her courage to find them.

Her knees were shaking with fear. Her baby jumped when Kitty heard a screaming cry that was so loud, she covered her ears with her hands.

"God, please help me find Carl and Robert." She cried out loud. Kitty looked down and saw the biggest footprint she had ever seen. She knew God was putting her on the right path. She followed the huge footprints that led to the cave near the waterfall.

Carl stopped in his track when he saw the giant bear in his path. He tried to run, but the long arm of the bear grabbed him and carried him to cave. Robert ran into his arms. His father hugged him. Carl knew Kitty would be worried sick when it got dark, and they we're not home. Stress like that could put her in labor early.

He rubbed his hands together. Thinking about the bears. They were intelligent, and they were kind to share their food. Carl thought he was dreaming when he heard her voice say, "Thank God, you both are saved."

Robert ran into his mother's arms, crying, "Mommy!"

Carl hugged them both. He whispers, "We are not safe." He pointed his finger at the huge bears.

One bear brought some berries over to them to eat. Kitty noticed that he had only one leg and walked with cane. When he saw her, he let out a loud cry. "Kitty!" Kitty knew he thought she was her great-grandmother.

The bears helped them home. A short trail that led up to their cabin. Robert waved goodbye.

When Grandmother saw them coming, she quickly gathered up her little men. "Let's go back to Ireland and find a castle to scare people."

Rose came over with some fresh bread. Kitty asked her if Bob was her real father. Rose told her that Carolina came to her and told her that she was going have a baby. "I promised her that I would never tell Bob the truth. Where did you get that beautiful red hair?" she asked Kitty. "Carolina knew it was Bob's baby."

Kitty smiled. "Bob and I had Carolina buried in The Kelly Cemetery. By the way, she's not in the grave, I WAS MURDERED. Someday may you can meet your other grandparents in Seattle. Kitty, what wrong?"

"Baby number six is coming," said Kitty. "I hope this is it."

Rose laughed. "Please don't tell Bob our secret."

Kitty had a beautiful baby girl with red hair. She told Carl she was done having babies. "I can't have a poke. No more kissing and fooling around."

Carl pulled out a little box. "It's time you have this."

Kitty cried when she saw the gold ring. Carl put on her finger and kissed her. "Kitty." He grinned at her. "Can I have a little poke."

Kitty jumped into his strong arms. He carried his bride to bed. "I have always loved you, Kitty."

"I love you too." Kitty was happy. She knew that Bob really was her father. Tomorrow, she was going to write down the stories of the secrets of the Kelly's family. And she knew many secrets. She thought, *But the leg and the gold?*

"Kitty stop thinking and please me," said Carl. "I can make our seventh child. Maybe you'd be lucky and have twins."

"Oh, shut up, Carl," said Kitty as she kissed him.

The End

ABOUT THE AUTHOR

Patsy Wallace have written poem since she was twelve. She has had many poems published. Writing is something that gets into your soul, and you can't stop. She lived in Washington, with her husband, Jerry.

They have four grown children and eight grandchildren. She hopes you enjoy her story as much as she has enjoyed writing it. She wants to thank you for reading her book, *The Kelly's Family Secrets*.

She hopes you will be able to read the next book, *Bigfoot's Leg is Found*.